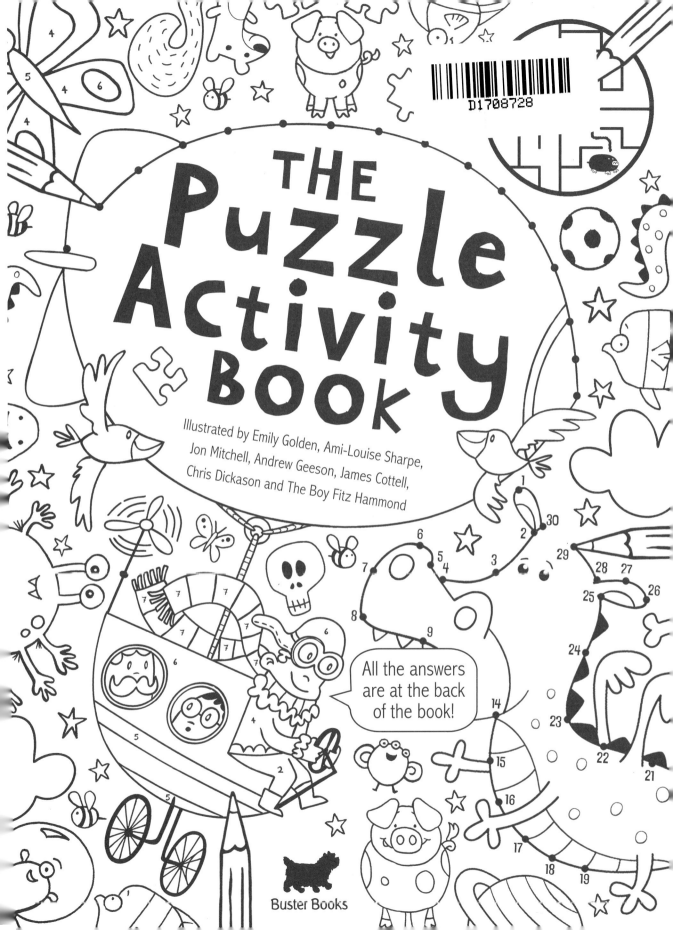

THE Puzzle Activity Book

Illustrated by Emily Golden, Ami-Louise Sharpe,
Jon Mitchell, Andrew Geeson, James Cottell,
Chris Dickason and The Boy Fitz Hammond

All the answers
are at the back
of the book!

Buster Books

Fill in the sections using the code below.
1 = brown   2 = blue   3 = pink
4 = yellow   5 = green   6 = orange

Which piece completes the jigsaw?
Can you draw it in?

Which kitten is unravelling the sock?

Can you spot the odd fish out in each shoal?

1

2

3

4

There are 10 differences between
these two magical scenes.

Can you spot and circle them all?

Join the dots and shade in the scene.

8

Match the hats to the correct shadows.

a

b

c

d

e

1

2

3

4

5

Can you spot 12 rabbits?

Circle the spider.

10

Spot the snail.

Colour the picture in.

There are 10 differences between
these two shop scenes.

Can you spot and circle them all?

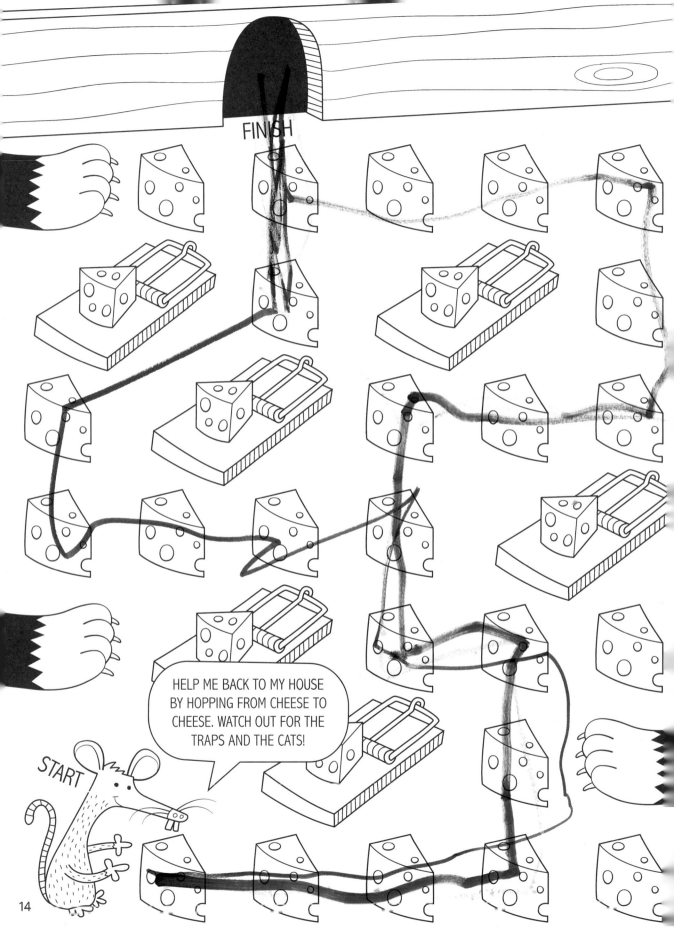

FINISH

HELP ME BACK TO MY HOUSE BY HOPPING FROM CHEESE TO CHEESE. WATCH OUT FOR THE TRAPS AND THE CATS!

START

14

Join the dots and shade in the scene.

29

30

1

2

28   27

3

26

4

25.

5

11   9

14   8

15   6
       7

12   10

24   16

13

17

23   18

22   19

20

21

Join the dots and shade in the scene.

Who scored a goal?

19

How many flowers
can you count?

20

Fill in this fun scene!

How many golf clubs are there?

Pair each animal with its baby.

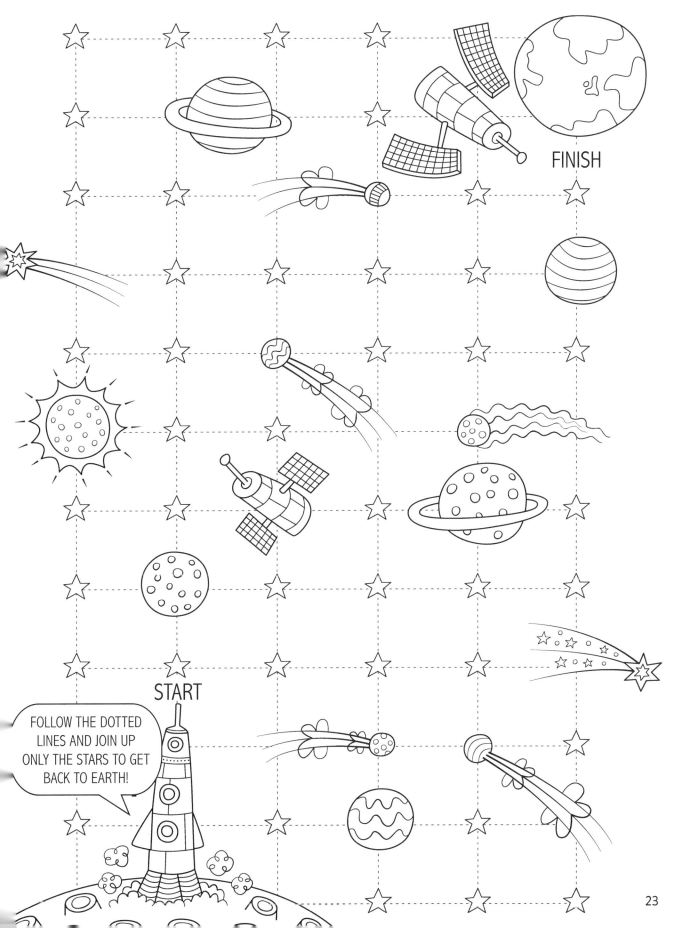

FINISH

START

FOLLOW THE DOTTED
LINES AND JOIN UP
ONLY THE STARS TO GET
BACK TO EARTH!

23

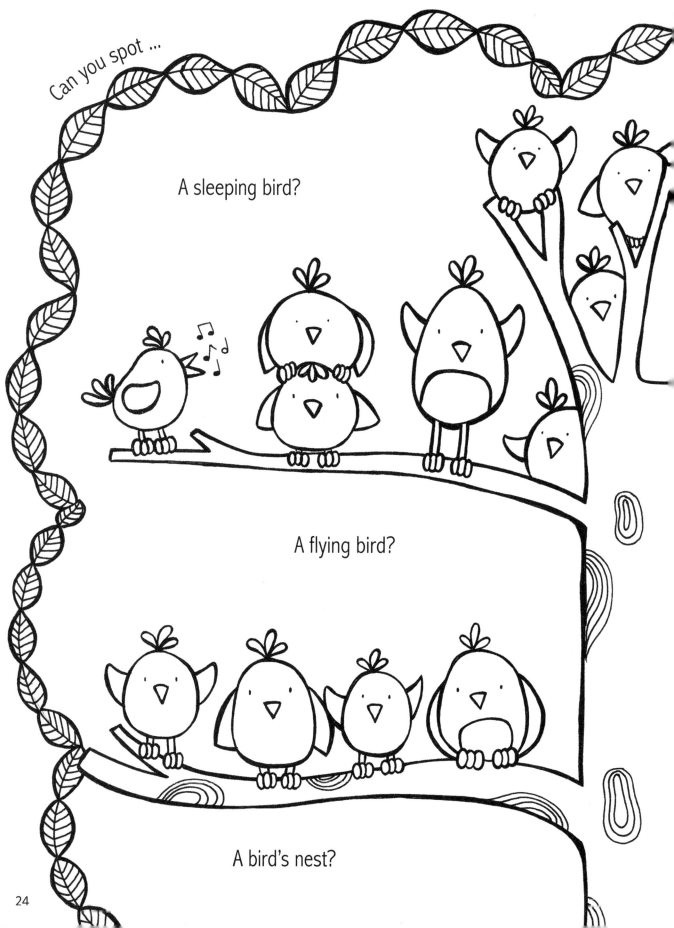

Can you spot ...

A sleeping bird?

A flying bird?

A bird's nest?

24

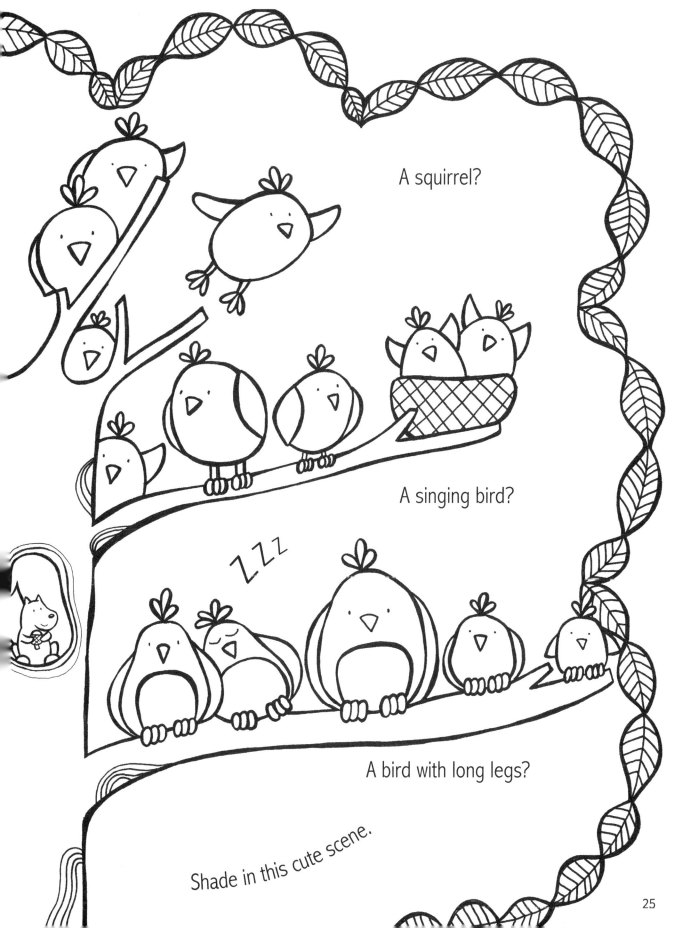

A squirrel?

A singing bird?

A bird with long legs?

Shade in this cute scene.

Which piece completes the jigsaw?
Can you draw it in?

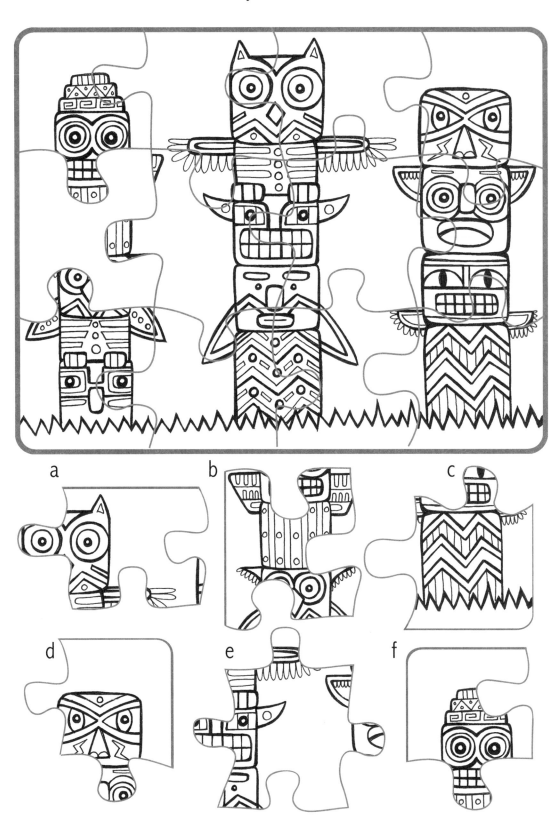

a

b

c

d

e

f

Match each kite to its shadow.

Who has hooked the boot?

a   b   c   d   e

Which piece completes the jigsaw?
Can you draw it in?

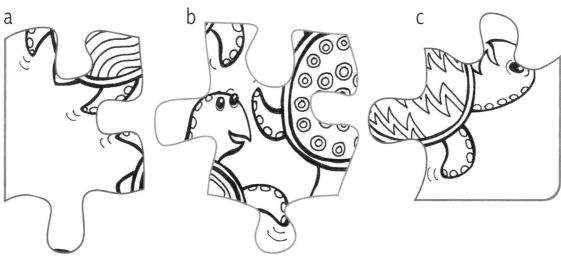

a b c

Find the two matching rows of flags.

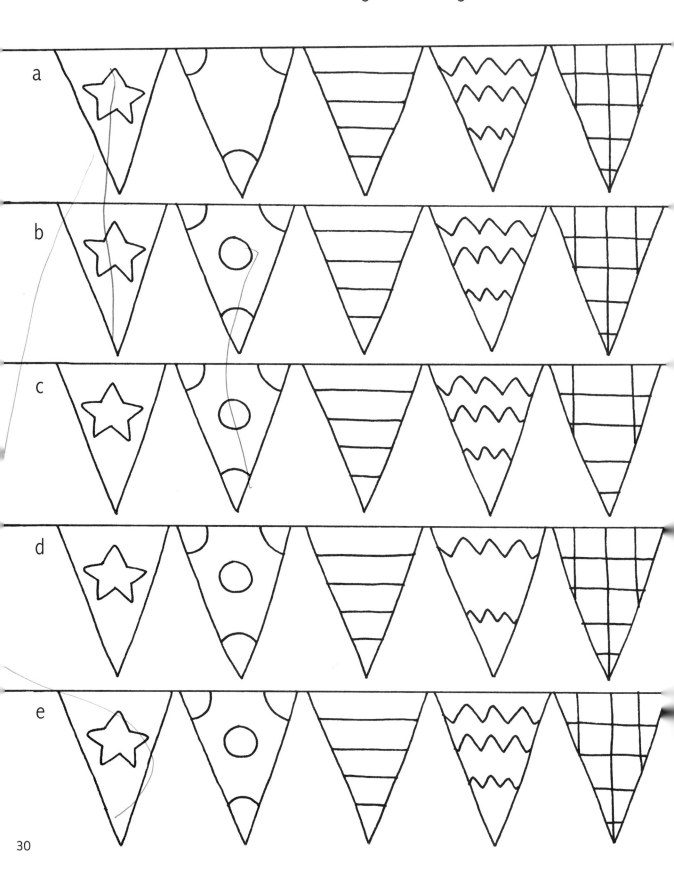

Can you put these dolls in size order, starting with the smallest?

Smallest

Biggest

a					

Can you spot ...

A spotty fish?

Some jewels?

A starfish?

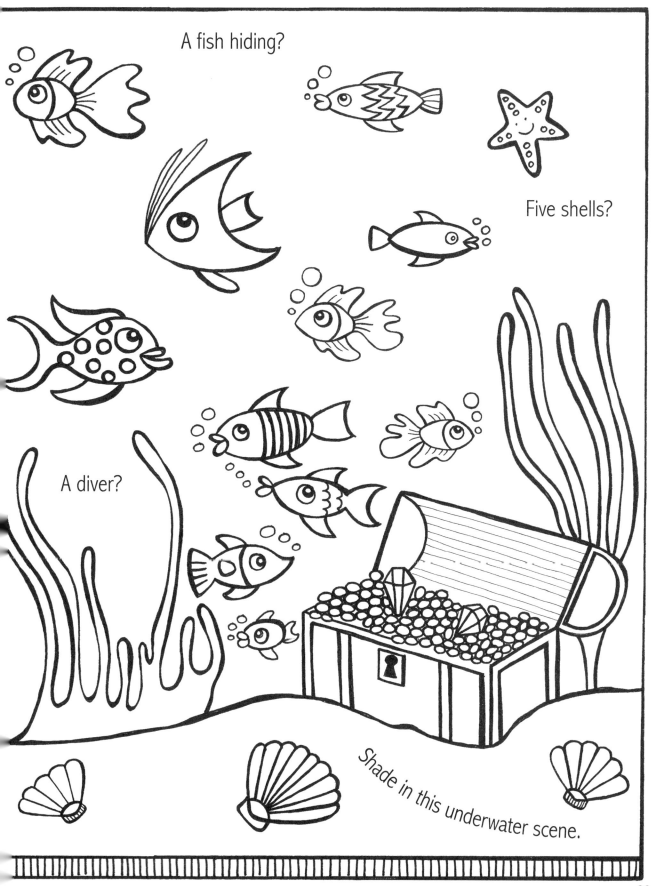

A fish hiding?

Five shells?

A diver?

Shade in this underwater scene.

33

Shade in the circus!

Can you spot ...

A strongman?

An umbrella?

Three clowns?

34

The ringmaster?

A fire-eater?

A juggler?

Shade in only the aliens with one eye!

Circle the alien with the most eyes.

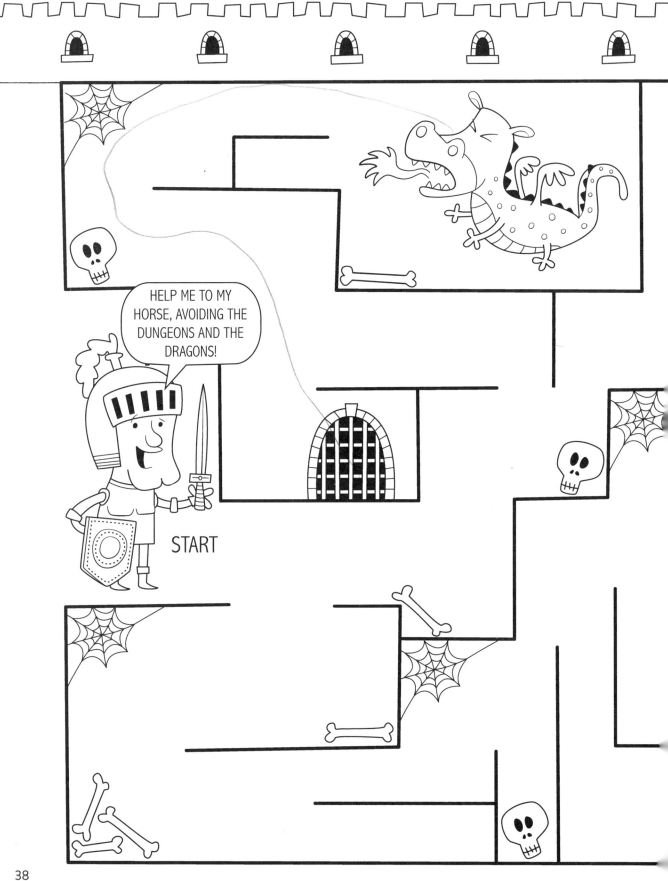

FINISH

There are 10 differences between these
two fun fancy-dress scenes.

Can you spot and circle them all?

Which piece completes the jigsaw?
Can you draw it in?

a

b

c

d

e

f

Which piece completes the jigsaw?
Can you draw it in?

a

b

c

FINISH

Can you shade in red the boats
with two people ...

... and the boats with three people in green?

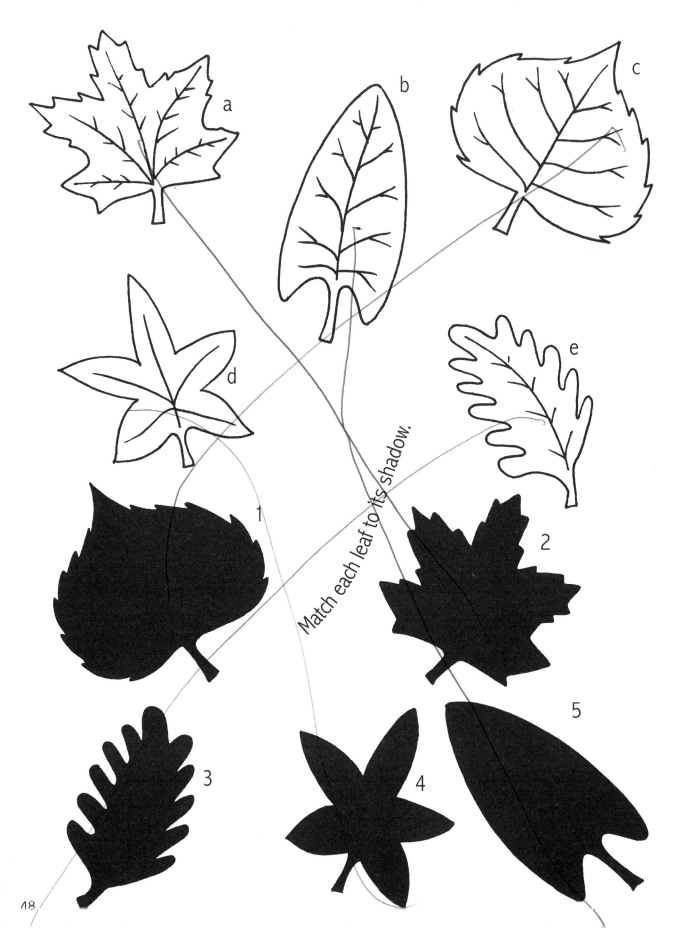

Match each leaf to its shadow.

48

Join the dots and shade in the scene.

49

Whose balloon is about to blow away?

SNAP!

Join the dots and shade in the scene.

51

There are 10 differences between
these two deep-sea scenes.

Can you spot and circle them all?

Can you spot ...

A boat?

A fish?

The sun?

54

A bucket
and spade?

A crab?

A beach ball?

Shade in the beach scene.

Link the matching bugs.
Add some spots to make the last one match!

Join the dots and shade in the scene.

There are 10 differences between
these two heroic scenes.

Fill in the sections using the code below.
1 = pink   2 = purple   3 = orange
4 = green   5 = yellow   6 = blue

All the answers

Page 3
Piece c completes the jigsaw

Page 4
Kitten c is unravelling the sock

Page 5
1 = c, 2 = b, 3 = b, 4 = a

Pages 6-7

Page 9
a = 2, b = 1, c = 4, d = 5, e = 3

Pages 10-11

Pages 12-13

Page 14

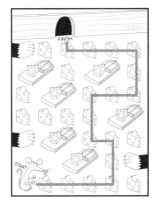

Pages 16-17

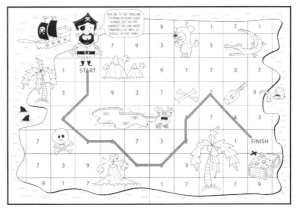

Page 19
Child e is scoring the goal

Pages 20-21
There are 16 flowers and 6 golf clubs

Page 30
Rows b and e match

Page 22
a = 1, b = 5, c = 3, d = 4, e = 2

Page 31
a, f, b, d, e, c

Page 23

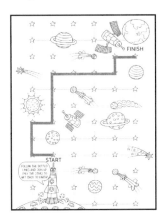

Pages 32-33

Pages 24-25

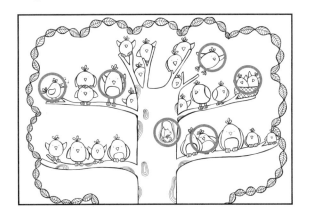

Pages 34-35

Page 26
Piece b completes the jigsaw

Page 27
a = 5, b = 2, c = 1, d = 4, e = 3

Page 28
Child e has hooked the boot

Page 29
Piece b completes the jigsaw

Pages 36-37

Pages 38-39

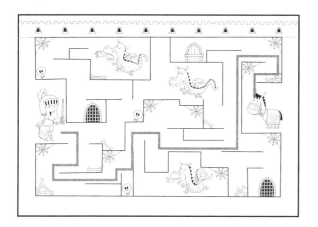

Pages 40-41

Page 42
Piece a completes the jigsaw

Page 43
Piece c completes the jigsaw

Pages 44-45

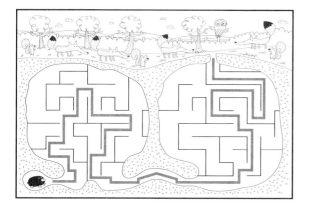

Pages 46-47
3 red boats

5 green boats

Page 48
a = 2, b = 5, c = 1, d = 4, e = 3

Page 50
Child d's balloon is about to blow away

Pages 52-53

Pages 54-55

Pages 58-59

Page 56
a = f, b = d, c = g,
e = add 6 spots to bug h

First published in 2015 by Buster Books,
an imprint of Michael O'Mara Books Limited,
9 Lion Yard, Tremadoc Road, London SW4 7NQ

The material in this book was taken from *The Big Busy Book* published by Buster Books.

W www.mombooks.com/buster
f Buster Books
Y @BusterBooks

A CIP catalogue record for this book is available from the British Library.

ISBN: 978-1-78055-313-9

12 14 16 18 20 19 17 15 13

This book was printed in October 2020 by
Leo Paper Products Ltd, Heshan Astros Printing Limited,
Xuantan Temple Industrial Zone, Gulao Town,
Heshan City, Guangdong Province, China.

MIX
Paper from
responsible sources
FSC® C020056
FSC
www.fsc.org